Spotlight Club Mysteries

•

THE MYSTERY OF THE SILVER TAG
THE MYSTERY OF THE MISSING SUITCASE
THE HIDDEN BOX MYSTERY
MYSTERY AT MACADOO ZOO
THE MYSTERY OF THE WHISPERING VOICE
THE MYSTERY OF THE MELTING SNOWMAN
MYSTERY OF THE BEWITCHED BOOKMOBILE
MYSTERY OF THE VANISHING VISITOR
MYSTERY OF THE LONELY LANTERN

A SPOTLIGHT CLUB MYSTERY

Mystery at Keyhole Carnival

Florence Parry Heide
and Roxanne Heide

Illustrations by Seymour Fleishman

ALBERT WHITMAN & Company · Chicago

Library of Congress Cataloging in Publication Data

Heide, Florence Parry, date
  Mystery at Keyhole Carnival.
  (A Splotlight Club mystery) (Pilot books series)
  SUMMARY: While working part-time at a carnival, the
Spotlight detectives discover a plot to keep the carnival
from staying in their town.
  [1. Mystery and detective stories] I. Heide,
Roxanne, joint author. II. Fleishman, Seymour.
III. Title.
PZ7.H36Myc   [Fic]   76-45426
ISBN 0-8075-5361-1

Contents

1 · Odd Jobs

THE TELEPHONE RANG and Jay Temple shouted, "Finally! I was beginning to feel unpopular."

"Let's cross our fingers," said Cindy, looking at her brother.

"Mine have been crossed all day," said Dexter Tate, Jay and Cindy's next door neighbor.

Jay cleared his throat and picked up the telephone. "Hello," he said in his deepest voice.

"Is this the party who had the ad in the paper for odd jobs?" asked a man. His voice was soft.

"Yes, sir," said Jay. He made the okay sign to Dexter and Cindy. "This is Jay Temple speaking."

"Well, I'd like to talk to you about an odd job. How soon could you come out?"

"Right away," said Jay. "May I have your address, please?"

"Keyhole Carnival," answered the man. "Just opened. Out on Route 31 and Hathaway, near that warehouse. I'm Sax Darby. I own the carnival. You can find me in the trailer behind the Ferris wheel. If I'm not there, I'll be manning a booth. Or operating one of the rides. Just ask around."

"Yes, Mr. Darby," said Jay.

"Call me Sax," the carnival owner put in.

"All right, Sax. Be out right away," said Jay.

"Not too soon. I have some work to do. I'll see you at . . . let's say at three o'clock."

"Fine," said Jay. He hung up the telephone. "The carnival! Keyhole Carnival," he said excitedly.

Dexter grinned. "Perfect!"

"I knew we'd be getting a job," said Cindy.

"We don't have it for sure," Jay reminded her.

"We will," Cindy answered confidently. She

picked up the newspaper and pointed to the ad that they had been running. "How could we miss?"

The ad read:

> ODD JOBS WANTED. Will clean garages, attics, basements. Wash windows, dishes, children. Baby-sit kids, pets, plants, fish. Run errands, mow lawns, trim edges and hedges. You name it, we'll do it. Call 652-7564. Reasonable rates.

"The only thing we didn't put in was 'We solve mysteries. The Spotlight Club at your service,'" said Dexter.

"Maybe we can do that next summer," said Jay. "When we're more famous."

"Well, let's go and have our interview," Dexter suggested.

"Mr. Darby—he says to call him Sax—is busy until three," said Jay.

"That's two hours from now," groaned Dexter. "I can't stand the suspense."

"There's no reason why we can't go out right now and look around," said Jay.

"Good," said Cindy. "We can learn our way around before we meet Sax."

Soon the Spotlighters were cycling along the highway to Keyhole Carnival.

"That's it, just ahead," called Jay over his shoulder. The three parked their bikes in the racks and stood looking up at the brightly lighted entrance. It was built in the shape of a huge keyhole, with small brass keys hanging from the top. Big lighted letters curved around the keyhole to spell WELCOME TO KEYHOLE CARNIVAL.

"I feel like Alice in Wonderland," said Cindy. "Small enough to walk through a keyhole."

The sun shone on the gaily decorated booths that stretched in front of the Spotlighters. Music blared through the loudspeakers.

The carnival rides were beyond the two parallel lines of booths. "There's the Ferris wheel," said Jay, pointing. "We'll find Sax Darby's trailer behind it."

"Ferris wheel," said Cindy, "my favorite ride. And the Hammer, my least favorite." She shuddered. "Your teeth nearly drop out of your head in one of those upside-down monsters."

The lane between the two lines of booths was filled with people of all ages carrying balloons, popcorn, cotton candy, and souvenirs.

"It's going to be great working here," said Dexter. "All the people, the hot dogs, the popcorn, the—"

"Whoa," Jay said. "We haven't got the job yet."

The Spotlighters walked along between the two lines of booths. Barkers called out, "Hey, spend a quarter, strike it rich!" and, "Give yourself a break. Break the record! Prizes galore!"

"Wonder what our job is?" asked Jay.

"Maybe it's blowing up balloons," suggested Dexter as a clown carrying dozens of bobbing balloons walked toward them.

"Balloons, get your balloons here, all colors, any color," chanted the clown. He waved to a girl who was walking ahead of the detectives. "Hey, Tracy!"

"Hey, Moon," the girl called back. Her long blond braids hung to her waist. She wore a bright red smock, and at the collar was pinned a brass key with the words "Keyhole Carnival" printed on it.

Tracy seemed to be popular. Other carnival workers waved and called out to her.

Suddenly Tracy whirled around. She said in surprise, "Why, Willie Kittles, what on earth are you doing here at this carnival?"

A big burly man wearing a wide-brimmed straw hat and a red bandanna around his neck grinned at Tracy. He was missing a front tooth, Cindy noted.

"I was just looking for you at your popcorn stand," Willie Kittles told the girl. "I've got to have a talk with you." He drew Tracy to one side, and the Spotlighters moved on.

The space between the two lines of booths grew narrower as the Spotlighters walked along.

"Popcorn Parlor," announced Dexter as they neared the last booths before the rides began. A red-and-white striped awning covered the stand.

"But no one's here to sell popcorn," said Jay.

Cindy remembered the girl named Tracy. Hadn't Kittles tried to find her at the popcorn stand?

Next to Popcorn Parlor was a ring-toss booth. A young man walked up and down in front of it. "Come on, try your luck!" he called. "Three fat juicy chances for one thin quarter!"

He saw the Spotlighters looking over at him. "Come on, take a chance!" he smiled at them. "Chances are you'll win one of these great prizes. Look—pillows, all kinds, all colors, all shapes and sizes!"

"I really like that big green one," Cindy said.

Could the young man at the booth be Sax Darby? Jay wondered. The carnival owner had said he sometimes manned a booth. "Are you Sax Darby?" Jay asked.

The young man smiled and shook his head. "No, but I wish I could be Sax, owning a great carnival like this. That's my main ambition in life. No, I'm not Sax. I'm only Chet Hamilton, hired help, ring-toss booth operator, and general handyman. And right now I'm selling popcorn on the side."

Dexter spoke up. "We don't want popcorn now, but we'd like to try for that green pillow."

"Right you are, sir," said Chet.

"I'll give it a try, too," Jay decided. The boys put down their quarters and picked up the rings as Tracy walked over to the popcorn stand.

"Tracy, where have you been?" called Chet. "You can't sell popcorn if you wander off."

"Well, I'm here now," called Tracy. She chewed her gum and started to fill popcorn boxes.

While the boys tried their luck with the ring-toss, Cindy walked over to the souvenir stand across the way. A pretty girl wearing a red smock was behind the counter. She smiled when she saw Cindy.

"Get your genuine Keyhole Carnival souvenirs right here," she said. "Absolutely guaranteed to cost more than they're worth."

Cindy blinked. The girl's green eyes were laughing.

"Nobody ever listens to what we call out, anyway," confided the girl, smoothing her short black curly hair. "I say all kinds of things and nobody notices."

Cindy saw that, like Tracy, this girl wore a brass key on her lapel. Under the key was her name card, Colleen.

Cindy smiled back. "It must be fun to work for a carnival."

"I'm not sure yet," said Colleen. "This is my first week. The only reason I'm here is that I happen to be madly in love with that lovable character across the way. And luckily, he happens to be in love with me. We're getting married pretty soon."

"You mean Chet Hamilton?" asked Cindy.

Colleen nodded. "Of course. Is there anyone else in the world?"

There was a loud wail from the popcorn booth.

15

Cindy glanced over. "Ooooh, Chet!" cried Tracy. "The popcorn machine isn't working. It was all right when I left, but it isn't now."

Colleen frowned. "Something else gone wrong? Oh, no."

Chet called over to Tracy from his ring-toss booth, "Just a minute. I'll be right there and fix it. These kids have one more toss."

"This is my last try," said Dexter. "Wish me luck, Cindy. It's your pillow, coming up!" He tossed and made it.

"Good work," said Chet admiringly. "The pillow is all yours." He handed it to Dexter. Then he called to Tracy, "Now here I come with my trusty toolbox. The popcorn machine is as good as fixed."

Dexter and Jay walked over to Colleen's souvenir stand. "All yours, Cindy," Dexter announced proudly, handing her the big green pillow. "That means you have to carry it."

Cindy made a face. "How can I apply for a job carrying a pillow that's bigger than I am?" she asked. "Sax Darby won't want to hire a big green pillow."

Colleen laughed. "Are you kids trying to get a

job here?" she asked. They nodded. "Oh, good. I wish you luck." Colleen turned to Cindy. "Why not leave the pillow here? I'll just keep it under the counter for you."

"Thanks," said Cindy. "I can pick it up later."

"I'll be dying to hear whether you get the job," said Colleen. "We can use some extra hands around here."

"We'll let you know," promised Cindy.

Suddenly there was a shout. Chet's stand was collapsing! In a moment the whole booth had fallen. It was a jumble of canvas and wood.

"Oh, oh!" wailed Tracy, wringing her hands.

"I don't believe it," whispered Colleen.

Chet ran from the popcorn stand over to his own booth. He stood staring at the crumpled stand.

Cindy, Jay, and Dexter ran to help Chet. They each took a side of the canvas and pulled. When it was up, Cindy darted around underneath to pick up pillows that had fallen. On the ground in front of her were the supports that had held up the canvas.

Suddenly Cindy stared. One of the supports had been neatly sawed through. It hadn't been an accident!

2 · Too Many Accidents

CINDY STARED at the sawed-through support. Some-one had done it on purpose. Someone meant it to look like an accident. Who? Why? Was someone mad at Chet?

Cindy kicked the support out of the way. Until she could find out the answers to *who* and *why,* she didn't want anybody else but Jay and Dexter to know about it. Not even Chet.

She stood up. Chet was saying, "Thanks, guys. I guess that's just about all we can do until I run over to the lumberyard and get some new supports."

"Tough luck," said Dexter.

Chet frowned. "It sure is. I won't have this stand back in shape for a couple of hours." He leaned down and picked up a big card on a string and hung it over the stand. "Closed" the sign read, "Try me later."

"Lumberyard, here I come," said Chet, starting to stride off through the crowd.

"When are you going to fix my popcorn machine?" wailed Tracy to Chet's back.

Cindy whispered to the boys, "We've got to talk." She walked toward the picnic tables placed in the center of the circle formed by the rides.

"Someone sawed part way through one of the supports," she told them. "So the whole thing was bound to collapse sooner or later just from the weight of the canvas."

"So it wasn't an accident," said Jay, frowning. "But it was supposed to look like one."

"Why?" asked Cindy. "Who would want to do anything to hurt Chet?"

"Or the carnival?" added Dexter. He looked at his watch. "We've got plenty of time before our appointment with Sax Darby. Let's grab a lemonade and sit down and think."

"I'll get the lemonade," said Jay. "You two find us a free table."

In a moment they were sitting at a table with their lemonade. Carnival noises were all around them. Music and the laughter of children hummed in the background.

Cindy took out her notebook. "We've got two reasons to learn all we can about Keyhole Carnival," she said. "One, the job. Two, the mystery." She wrote busily.

Jay peered over her shoulder. "What are you doing?" he asked.

"Making a diagram," explained Cindy. "So we can remember where everything is."

In a moment she tilted her head and looked at her drawing. "Look, the whole carnival is in the shape of a huge keyhole!" she said.

"If something funny is going on, we've got to know as much as we can about the carnival. And its people," said Dexter, pushing his glasses down on his nose.

Cindy turned a page. "People," she said to herself. She wrote, *Owner:* Sax Darby. *Staff Members* (so far): Chet—ring-toss, Colleen—souvenir stand,

Tracy—popcorn stand. *Remarks:* Chet and Colleen are going to be married.

Cindy looked up at the boys. "That's all we know. So far." She thought a moment. "Tracy was talking to that man with the big hat and the red bandanna," she said. "His name is Kittles. But he doesn't work here."

"How do you know?" asked Jay.

"Because when Tracy saw him she was surprised," Cindy said. "She wanted to know what he was doing here at *this* carnival. So I think he must work for another carnival."

"Put his name down," suggested Dexter. "We can find out more about him later."

Cindy added to her notebook. Under *Other People,* she wrote: Kittles (Works for another carnival?) Then she turned a page. She wrote, *Mystery:* Support for Chet's stand sawed through. Supposed to look like accident. Wasn't.

"Shouldn't we tell Chet that it was done on purpose?" asked Dexter. "Or maybe we should tell Sax Darby when we meet him?"

Jay scratched his head. "We shouldn't tell anyone anything yet," he decided. "We really don't know anything yet. We might be telling the person who did it, for all we know."

"All right," agreed Cindy. "Let's not say anything to anyone until we have more facts." She added thoughtfully, "Colleen said other things have been going wrong. And now the popcorn machine is broken, too."

Suddenly Dexter glanced at his watch. "Hey! It's three o'clock! Time to find Sax Darby!"

They put their paper cups in one of the bright red trash cans and headed for Sax Darby's trailer.

"There it is," said Jay, pointing to a small trailer. Stars were painted on the door and on the sides. Flowers in pots lined the windows.

"I like this trailer," whispered Cindy as Jay knocked on the gaily painted door. The door opened.

In the doorway stood a young woman. She was slender, and her dark hair was pulled back from her face to make a long ponytail.

"Hello, hello, hello," she said. "Three hellos for three people. Sax," she called over her shoulder. "When we have children, let's call one of them Hello. It has such a lovely sound."

She turned back to the Spotlighters. "I'm Marra Darby. Come in. Without even knowing who you are, I like you. You give me good vibes."

They followed her into a small cluttered living room.

A young man sat on the floor. Piles of papers and notebooks surrounded him. Cindy noted that he was dressed exactly like Marra: blue jeans, sandals, and a bright red shirt. His long hair was tied back the same way. They both wore silver bracelets and rings, and silver chains around their necks.

"Sax darling, here's company," Marra said eagerly. "To take your mind off all the bad things that have been happening."

Sax looked up and smiled. "Hi. I'm Sax Darby. Are you enjoying the carnival? Anything I can do for you?"

"I talked to you on the telephone," said Jay. "About the job. We'd like to apply."

Sax raised his dark eyebrows. "I wasn't expecting so many of you. One person could do the job. But perhaps three would be better, after all."

"Three is a calm, peaceful number," said Marra. She walked into the tiny kitchen that was at one end of the living room. She started to stir an enormous pot on the stove. "Sax, I feel very good about these people. Hire them."

Sax smiled at her. Then he looked around him at the papers on the floor. "I'm sorry about this mess. All my payroll checks that I was going to sign are missing. All the time sheets, all the work charts. Everything has disappeared." He fingered one of the silver chains around his neck. "I must find those checks, I must. I have to sign them. I was to pay everybody today. They're all counting on it. And now I won't be able to have the checks ready in time."

Marra walked over to Sax and put her hand on his shoulder. "It's no good to fret," she said. "Fretting only dampens the electricity in your system and makes you short out."

In spite of Sax's worried frown, his eyes smiled. "Everything was right here on my desk last night when we went to see your sister," he said. "We never lock the door. Anyone could have taken the stuff. But why? Unsigned checks, time sheets—nothing that would do anyone any good. I can't understand it."

24

Cindy frowned. Who could have done this? Maybe the same person who had sawed the support for Chet's stand? But why?

Sax turned to the Spotlighters. "About the job," he said. "It isn't really much of a job. It's picking up litter. You know, candy wrappers, paper

cups, popcorn boxes, things like that. People drop them all over the grounds instead of in the trash containers. Your job will be to pick everything up and put it into the containers." He paused. "That is, if you want the job."

"We do want the job," said Jay.

"Then it's yours," said Sax.

Marra clapped her hands. "We need good vibes around here!"

"Could you start tomorrow?" asked Sax. Jay, Cindy, and Dexter nodded.

"Great. Marra and I want Keyhole Carnival to look neat."

Marra returned to the pot on the stove and started to stir. "Especially now," she said. "Tell them why it's so important, Sax."

Sax turned one of his bracelets. "The town is considering having a permanent carnival here. In the past there would be one or two carnivals setting up for a week or so. What Kenoska wants now is a permanent amusement park. It would be wonderful for us if the Park Committee decided to keep Keyhole Carnival here. Usually we move around from town to town."

"I always feel the towns are moving around us," said Marra, stirring the big pot.

"We really need to make a good impression," Sax went on. "The Park Committee is sending someone over to inspect us, to decide if we're worthy of being here permanently."

"I know these new friends will do all they can to make our carnival the best," put in Marra. "To make it better than Kittles' Carnival."

Cindy frowned. Kittles. The man who had been talking to Tracy, the man with the red bandanna, must own Kittles' Carnival.

"That awful Kittles," pouted Marra. "He left a bad feeling this morning when he came to talk to you, Sax. He was so mad about your hiring that Tracy girl away from him."

"I didn't hire Tracy away from Kittles," said Sax. "I told Kittles that. She applied for the job and I gave it to her."

"I don't like that man Kittles," said Marra. "I don't trust anyone with pointed ears."

"Pointed ears," laughed Sax. "He doesn't have pointed ears, Marra."

"You may not see them, but I do," said Marra.

She smiled at Cindy, Jay, and Dexter. "I see invisible things," she confided.

"Marra's a little wizard at heart," said Sax.

"Not a wizard, Sax, a witch," corrected Marra. "A good witch. That's how I know about Kittles. There will be trouble as long as he's around," she predicted darkly. "I bet he sneaked in here last night and took all those records, Sax, just to cause trouble."

"Oh, Marra," said Sax. "Because you don't like Kittles, it doesn't mean he'd do anything like that."

"A bad person does bad things," said Marra.

Cindy looked over at Jay and Dexter meaningfully. Was it Kittles? Had he sawed the support? Had he taken Sax's records?

Sax turned to the three detectives. "Kittles is the owner of another carnival," he explained. "He's angry because we got our carnival into Kenoska. He had to settle for having his in that little town of Willette. And now he's doubly angry because we're here, first in line to be considered as the permanent carnival. He thinks his carnival should be chosen. He's been in the business a lot longer than we have, and he does know a lot about carnivals."

He thought for a moment. "You know, we're pretty shorthanded right now. Since there are three of you, maybe you could fill in when you're needed. You look old enough. Help sell tickets, maybe, or help man a stand, things like that."

"Great," said Dexter.

"Then we'll see you tomorrow," said Sax. "The carnival opens at noon, if you'll be here by then, please."

Cindy asked, "How late do you want us to work?" She knew her mother wouldn't let them work late at night.

Marra gazed at one of her rings. "This girl knows her mother wouldn't want them to work too late at night," she said.

Cindy was startled. Was Marra a mind reader?

"You won't have to work past six," Sax assured them. "We have a night watchman. Hil likes to come early and keep busy."

"You should say night watchperson," said Marra.

Sax smiled. He turned to the three Spotlighters. "You'll get acquainted with everyone soon. Look around. If you have any questions, ask me or ask Chet. He has the ring-toss booth next to the popcorn stand. Chet knows as much about this carnival as I do. More. In fact, he wants to buy it from me. But I'll never sell. Never."

"Maybe if you did sell to Chet, you wouldn't have so many worries," Marra said. "We don't need to own this carnival. If you own things, you own worries."

"Owning this carnival is more important to me than anything in the world," said Sax firmly. "Except you, Marra." He smiled gently at her.

Cindy was thinking how much fun it would be to be part of this carnival. Part of the staff. She wondered whether she would wear a red smock like Tracy's and Colleen's.

Marra turned to Cindy. "You won't want to bother with the red smocks," she said. "You'll be all right in easy clothes, like the ones you're wearing."

Cindy blinked. *Was* Marra a mind reader?

Marra blew them a kiss as the Spotlighters walked away from the trailer.

3 · Who's Making Trouble?

CINDY, JAY, AND DEXTER walked thoughtfully toward the whirling rides. The music grew loud as they drew near.

"We've got a job!" said Jay. "A summer job!"

"And a mystery," Cindy reminded him.

"Carnivals always make me hungry," said Dexter. "Let's stop and have a hot dog. Besides, we need a chance to think things through. Somebody sawed that support of Chet's. And somebody took Sax's records."

Soon the detectives were sitting at one of the picnic tables, eating.

Cindy opened her notebook and glanced at what she had already written. Under *Owner,* she added Marra below Sax Darby. Under *Staff,* she added Night Watchman: Hil.

"Add us," suggested Jay. "We're staff now."

Cindy wrote, "Dexter, Jay, Cindy—Ground-keepers."

"That's a pretty great title," said Jay.

"We're a pretty great crew," said Dexter.

Cindy chewed her pencil. "I'm going to make a list of all the things Kittles has done to Keyhole Carnival," she said.

Jay laughed. "Talk about jumping to conclusions! We don't know it's Kittles."

"Remember Mr. Hooley's Rule," said Dexter. "We have to prove what we suspect."

"All right," agreed Cindy. "Let's prove Kittles did all these things. The popcorn machine. The support to Chet's stand. Sax's records. And there is more that we don't even know about. Colleen said things have been happening."

"Let's ask her," suggested Dexter, taking a last bite of hot dog.

As the three detectives walked toward Colleen's

stand, they saw that Chet was back from the lumberyard. He was already at work on the repairs to his own stand.

"Let's give him a hand, Jay," suggested Dexter.

"I'll talk to Colleen while you help Chet," offered Cindy. "I'll find out everything I can about this Kittles."

Cindy leaned over the counter of Colleen's souvenir stand. A little girl pulled at her mother's dress. "I don't want a souvenir," she whined. "I want popcorn."

"The popcorn machine is broken," said her mother. "We'll get a nice souvenir instead."

"I want popcorn," pouted the little girl.

"Kids!" Colleen exclaimed. Turning angrily she said, "Listen, you spoiled little brat. There's no popcorn, okay? So you don't want a souvenir. That's okay, too. Why don't you just go home and have a good cry?"

The child opened her mouth, but not a sound came out.

Cindy bent down toward the little girl. "Hey, there's a neat merry-go-round over there. You can ride on the black horse if you hurry."

The little girl looked at Cindy. Then she pulled at her mother. "I wanna ride the merry-go-round."

The mother smiled gratefully at Cindy and went off with the child.

Colleen looked at Cindy and shook her head. "Now there's a good trick. Get their attention on something else. Then they forget the thing they're thinking about. I'll have to remember that one. I just get mad." She leaned on the counter. "Did you get the job?"

Cindy answered, "We're going to be the groundkeepers."

"Congratulations," said Colleen. "The keepers of the grounds. Maybe you'll bring Keyhole Carnival good luck. It sure needs some."

Cindy spoke quickly, "Remember when you said that things had been going wrong?"

"I don't remember saying it, but it's true. So many things have gone wrong this week. For instance, day before yesterday when the operator started the merry-go-round, he noticed one of the horses was loose. If he hadn't seen that, the horse might have fallen off."

Cindy frowned.

Colleen went on, "You haven't heard the rest. Yesterday morning the whole canvas cover on the caterpillar ride came off. Just as soon as the operator started it. Sax was positive he'd checked everything the night before, but—" She glanced over at Tracy's popcorn stand. "Now the popcorn machine. And Chet's stand."

"It sounds like a run of really bad luck," said Cindy.

"Bad luck?" repeated Colleen. "Maybe and maybe not."

"What do you mean?" asked Cindy, blinking.

Colleen glanced at Cindy and looked back at Chet's stand. "Why, I mean it might not be bad luck, just bad management. If Chet owned this carnival, things like this would never happen. I *know* that," she said positively. "Maybe if there are more accidents, Sax will get discouraged and sell out to Chet."

Did Colleen hope there would be more accidents? Cindy wondered. Just so that Sax would sell the carnival to Chet? Cindy shook her head. Of course not. Just because she was a detective, she didn't have to suspect everybody. Or did she? She made a mental note to jot down two other things which had gone wrong. The horse on the merry-go-round. The canvas top of the caterpillar ride.

Colleen looked behind Cindy and smiled brightly. "May I help you?" she asked. Several new customers had walked up to the stand to look at souvenirs.

Cindy started to walk over to Chet's ring-toss booth. The boys were still working on the repairs. Cindy paused. She could see a man with a wide-brimmed straw hat and a bright red bandanna walking her way. It was Kittles. With him was a tall, dignified looking man with gray hair. He wore a light gray business suit, a white shirt, and a narrow black tie. He looked as neat as Kittles looked untidy.

Kittles was steering the man to Chet's booth. Jay and Dexter held up the canvas while Chet pounded.

"See, Mr. McCoy?" asked Kittles. "Now this kind of thing could never happen at my carnival. Never has and never will. I run a tight ship."

The man called Mr. McCoy stroked his chin. "Well, Kittles, accidents can happen to the best of us. I know from experience in my own warehouse."

"But that ain't all, Mr. McCoy," Kittles went on. "The popcorn machine—"

"I'm not interested in gossip," Mr. McCoy interrupted. "I am here to see for myself how this carnival is run. I am the one who will make the report to the Park Committee, Mr. Kittles, not you."

Cindy thought quickly. This Mr. McCoy must be the representative that Sax had told the Spotlighters about. The one who was going to decide if Keyhole Carnival would stay in Kenoska permanently. And Kittles was trying to turn Mr. McCoy against Keyhole Carnival.

Mr. McCoy started to leave Kittles.

"But Mr. McCoy!" sputtered Kittles.

"I must make sure on my own, Mr. Kittles, how clean and how safe this carnival is," said Mr. McCoy firmly. "I do not need, and I will not accept, advice from the owner of a competing carnival. And now if you'll excuse me, I want to look at the rides before I return to my warehouse."

Mr. McCoy went toward the circle of rides.

"Good for Mr. McCoy," Cindy said to herself. "He won't listen to Kittles." She frowned. "But he's bound to see for himself how many things are going wrong here. We've got to help Sax. We've got to."

When Chet's stand was repaired, Cindy began to help the boys and Chet put the scattered pillows back.

"Thanks a billion, kids," said Chet. He turned to Cindy. "The boys tell me that you three start working here tomorrow. As far as I can see, you've started today. Welcome aboard!"

"Hey, Chet," called Tracy from the popcorn stand. "Come and fix this machine now, will you? It's more important than your old stand."

Chet grinned at the Spotlighters. "Coming, your majesty!" he called.

Cindy drew the boys aside. Quickly she told them about what else had gone wrong at Keyhole Carnival. The loose horse on the merry-go-round. The canvas top on the caterpillar ride. "And Kittles brought Mr. McCoy over to see Chet's stand. You were too busy helping Chet to notice."

"Who's Mr. McCoy?" asked Jay.

"He's the one who's supposed to decide whether Keyhole Carnival is safe and clean enough to stay permanently in Kenoska. Kittles is trying to turn Mr. McCoy against Keyhole Carnival." She paused and took a breath. "But Mr. McCoy won't listen to Kittles. He wants to judge for himself."

Jay frowned. "It does look as if Kittles is the one who's arranging all these accidents," he said.

"We have to have proof," Dexter reminded them. "Just because he's the only one who has a motive doesn't mean he's the one who's doing it. There may be other people with other motives that we don't know anything about yet." He glanced at his watch. "Maxwells' patio blocks! We promised we'd get the rest laid by suppertime."

The three detectives ran for their bikes. By suppertime they had helped Mr. Maxwell place the last of his patio blocks. Randy and Amy Maxwell were hopping around watching.

"Mom's taking us to the carnival tomorrow," said Randy.

"Look for us. We'll be working there," Dexter said.

"And working on a new mystery," added Cindy under her breath as the Spotlighters headed home.

4 · Marra, the Mind Reader

AT NOON the next day, Anne dropped the three detectives at the carnival entrance.

"Thanks, Anne," said Dexter. "If I'd waited for my bike chain to get fixed, I'd have been late for work."

"That's okay," Anne said. "Sisters are allowed to do favors for brothers *once* in a while." She laughed. "Mike and I will pick your bike up at Don Gilly's when it's fixed. And we'll pick you kids up after our date."

"Great," Dexter said. The Spotlighters waved as Anne drove off.

"We're going to have lots of spare time tonight," said Jay. "Chet told me that the carnival closes early on Thursdays because it's open late on Fridays. And today's Thursday."

"Too bad, the one night we can stay late the carnival closes early," sighed Cindy.

The Spotlighters hurried through the Keyhole entrance. A young man with cameras and flash attachments hanging from his shoulders was just ahead of them. Under a straw hat, his shaggy blond hair stuck out in all directions.

"Tourist," whispered Dexter under his breath.

The man strode quickly ahead and was soon out of sight, his cameras swinging.

"Why are two cameras better than one?" wondered Cindy.

As the Spotlighters approached the souvenir booth they saw the man with the cameras talking to Colleen. They could see that his hat had a little card stuck in the band. It read *Press.*

"Newspaper photographer, not tourist," whispered Dexter.

The young man handed Colleen his card. "Skip Bannerman, of the Kenoska News," he announced. "I'm doing a feature series on Keyhole Carnival." He pulled his ear. "My headline for the spread is

'Will Kenoska Get Keyhole Carnival for Keeps?' I'll be taking lots of pictures. How about one of you here at the souvenir stand, just for starters?"

Colleen glanced at Cindy and winked. "Why not?" she asked. She posed leaning over her counter surrounded by souvenirs. Skip Bannerman took a flash picture. "Now what's a good caption for that picture?" he muttered. " 'Pretty Girl Mans Souvenir Stand,' maybe." He wrote in a little notebook.

Dexter nudged Cindy. "You're not the only one with a notebook today," he whispered.

"And that looks like a fun job, too," Cindy whispered back.

"Speaking of jobs," said Jay, "We'd better report to Sax so we can start work."

Cindy looked around. "Maybe he wants us to take tickets or something. There isn't much litter yet."

They found Sax, and he gave them their assignments. Taking tickets, helping keep the children in line at the rides, and picking up litter. "You can keep your eyes open," Sax told them. "Fill in where you see you're needed."

Suddenly the carnival was crowded with people

of all ages. They walked up and down the line of booths, ran toward the rides, bought popcorn, and played the games. And just as suddenly, thought Cindy, the carnival grounds were filled with litter. There were big red trash cans all over the grounds. Why weren't people ashamed to throw paper and empty popcorn boxes on the ground?

Up ahead there was a flash. Cindy saw Skip Bannerman. He was taking pictures of the crowd.

Just as Cindy had decided that she had picked up her ninety-ninth popcorn box, Jay came running up.

"I just saw Sax. Here's the latest accident." He paused for breath. "The sound system is out of order."

Cindy realized for the first time that there was no music coming over the loudspeakers.

"Sax is trying to fix it," Jay continued, panting. "He asked me to come and get Chet. Chet knows more about sound systems than Sax does."

Jay raced across to Chet's stand. In a moment Cindy saw Chet running, his toolbox in hand. Jay was on his heels.

Skip Bannerman posed an old man with a little

boy carrying a balloon. His flash went off. "'Balloons and Spirits Soar at Keyhole Carnival,'" he muttered. "'Old and Young Find Carnival Fun!'"

Cindy felt a tug on her sleeve. It was Amy Maxwell, and Randy was by her side.

"I won it with nobody else," Amy squealed excitedly, thrusting her clenched fist up to Cindy. "Just me. I won it." She opened her fist. A tiny key lay in her smudged hand.

"Good for you, Amy," Cindy said with a smile.

"And we got our picture taken." Randy added proudly, "With grown-ups."

"The balloon man!" Amy said happily.

"And once with a big lady," Randy added.

"I got my balloon for free, but it went bang," Amy said, squinting.

"And once with somebody with a watch, too," Randy went on.

"Yes, yes, yes, the peek watch," Amy squealed.

"Pink watch?" Cindy asked.

"No, no, no, a *peek* watch," Amy insisted. "It opens and shuts and it makes me laugh." She giggled. "I saw it more than Randy did."

"Did not," Randy said.

"Did too," Amy said.

"Did not," Randy said again.

"Did too," Amy said firmly.

Cindy looked around and saw Mrs. Maxwell, sitting on a bench, watching Amy and Randy. She caught Cindy's eye and waved.

Meanwhile, Jay was walking near the Ferris wheel. He leaned down and picked up one more paper cup. He wondered if all the bright red trash cans were invisible to everyone. They must be, he decided. Maybe Sax should put blinking lights on the trash cans so people would see them.

He glanced up and saw Kittles and Mr. McCoy. Both men were again looking around the carnival.

"Listen, Mr. McCoy, you hear any music? It's broken, that's why. People at carnivals expect good, loud music."

Mr. McCoy spoke coldly. "Some of us prefer quiet," he said, and walked on.

Jay grinned. He saw what Cindy meant when she said Mr. McCoy could handle Kittles.

Jay frowned suddenly. Mr. McCoy was sure to be thinking about Chet's fallen stand and the broken popcorn machine and the fact that now the sound system wasn't working. Mr. McCoy didn't need Kittles to tell him that things were going wrong at Keyhole Carnival.

Jay kept picking up paper plates and napkins and popcorn boxes, but his mind was on the mystery.

Kittles was trying to ruin Keyhole Carnival by *talking* against it—but was that all he was guilty of? Was he also arranging the accidents?

Jay glanced up when he heard Marra's lilting laugh. She was pulling on Sax's arm as they walked along. "Sax, it's a perfect time to let me do my act. You promised I could."

Sax saw Jay and nodded his head. "You're doing a good job. And Dexter's over there selling tickets to the Tilt-a-whirl. When you get tired doing the litter bit, trade places with him. I told him the same about you."

Jay smiled. "We really like it here, Sax," he said.

"Good," said Sax, glancing around. "It looks as though I'll have to man the Big Bonger today. Kittles talked our regular man into joining his carnival. He just walked out, leaving me holding the bag." He turned to Jay. "Just tell people I'll be right back. I've got to talk to Chet."

"But Sax, forget about the Big Bonger," Marra said. "Everyone else will if you just let me stay here and do my act. It's much more exciting than any old bonger thing." She pulled at Sax's arm again. "You promised I could do my mind-reading act, you promised."

Sax looked at Marra and smiled. "Well, okay," he said. His smile faded. "I've got to talk to Chet. It's extremely important and I'd just as soon get it out of the way." He patted Marra's arm. "So while I'm over at his stand, you can read all the minds you want, okay?"

Jay wondered what was important about talking to Chet. Had anything else gone wrong?

Just then Marra clapped her hands. Jay raised his eyebrows. A mind-reading act? What next?

Marra tilted her head and looked up to the top of the Big Bonger. "Stupid thing," she said. "That's just for people to test their strength. They don't realize that the only strength that counts is in your heart and in your head."

She saw Jay and laughed delightedly. "I really do have special powers, you know," she told him. "I concentrate on the electricity in people and between people. I think of the colors in the electricity and the prettier the colors are, the better the vibes are." She blinked eagerly. "Let me try it out on you."

Jay swallowed. "I really should—"

"No, wait. If I think about the colors long enough, they form a word. Like your name, for instance." She closed her eyes. "It's Jay Temple!" she cried happily.

"But you already knew my name," Jay said.

"Well, that's true," Marra said, tilting her head. Her long black hair swung around. "I was just giving you an example."

"Oh," Jay said.

"I'm best when there's a crowd around me," Marra whispered. "You'd think the colors would get all mixed up and turn brown, but they don't. They just get thicker. Thick bands of color spelling out names, places, ages, all sorts of things." Her eyes glowed.

Jay cleared his throat. "Well. That sounds great." Actually, the last thing in the world he wanted was for anybody to read his mind. He'd have to get out of here, he—

"If you don't want me to read your mind, all right," pouted Marra. "I'll read that nice photographer's mind."

Jay turned to see Skip Bannerman coming toward them, his cameras swinging.

"I'll have to study him first," Marra whispered to Jay, stepping back. "To get his vibes."

"The Big Bonger is next on my list." Skip told Jay, who was in his way. "I've got a system now. I'm working all the way around the circle." He glanced up to the top of the Big Bonger and pulled on his ear. Then he swung his camera up and looked through it. "'Will Keyhole Carnival Make It to the Top?' 'Does Keyhole Carnival Know Its Own Strength?' No . . . let's see." He turned to Jay. "Want to try it out, for the picture?"

Jay looked at the mallet resting on the ground. "Sure," he grinned. He picked up the heavy mallet and raised it over his shoulder. "I'll never be able to ring the bell at the top," he thought.

Skip lifted his camera. "I'd like to shoot the picture as you swing the hammer down, okay?"

Jay nodded and swung the mallet down hard. He watched as the metal disc rose a few feet up the bonger. Then he gasped. It looked as if the tall iron structure was rocking.

"One more try, son," Skip was saying. "My flash didn't work."

Jay frowned and raised the mallet. He watched again as he swung down, not as hard this time. His eyes hadn't fooled him. The entire iron structure swayed slightly back and forth.

Jay's eyes darted to the base. He stared. His heart pounded as he stepped back. One of the large iron bolts supporting the bonger was missing. If he had hit one more time, the whole thing would have fallen.

Maybe it would anyway.

5 · Meeting Hil

JAY GLANCED AROUND quickly. Skip Bannerman was getting his camera ready for another shot. Customers, attracted by the picture taking, were walking up to the Big Bonger.

Jay's heart pounded. If the bonger fell, someone would be hurt. He'd have to keep people away. He didn't want anyone to panic. He glanced about hurriedly. Luckily there were only a few people standing near the bonger.

Jay made a quick decision. He turned to Skip. "I know you want to take pictures of all the rides," he said. "But Marra Darby, the wife of the owner, has an act you won't want to miss. Come on!"

He turned, grabbed Marra's hand, and led her quickly away from the bonger. He had to get the people to follow.

"Oh, dear," said Marra. "Just as I was getting into the reporter's mind. Now you've jerked it all away."

Jay glanced over his shoulder at the Big Bonger and the crowd nearby.

"Come one, come all," he shouted, and people's heads turned. "The one and only Marra! Marra the Mind Reader! Get your minds read now, folks! Right this way, ladies and gentlemen, follow me!"

Skip Bannerman, grinning, was right at their heels. Marra's eyes glowed. Jay looked back and saw with relief that he had led everyone away from the Big Bonger.

Jay called loudly, "Here you are, ladies and gentlemen! Presenting Marra, the mysterious, marvelous mind reader."

Mara stretched out her arms to the crowd. She said in a low voice, "Yes, I am Marra, and I will read your minds. Come closer."

More people gathered. Skip took pictures. Jay's plan had worked. Now he had to get Sax. He had to warn him about the bonger. It had to be repaired—now.

Jay backed away and sped to Chet's booth. Sax was talking earnestly to Chet. "Sax!" shouted Jay.

Sax looked around and began to say, "What's the—?"

"It's the bonger," interrupted Jay. He spoke softly so that no one else could hear. "A bolt is missing. It can fall. Hurry! It's dangerous."

Sax stared at Jay. Then he wheeled around and called to Chet. "Hurry! Bring your toolbox."

Chet moved fast. He grabbed his toolbox from under the counter.

Jay and Sax ran toward the Big Bonger. Chet was right behind them. As soon as they got to the bonger, Chet opened his toolbox and started to work.

"Sax," said Jay. "These aren't accidents. Someone is doing it all on purpose."

Sax shook his head. "That can't be! I have no enemies."

Chet called to Jay, "Go back and watch my stand for me, will you? I'll get back as soon as possible."

Jay nodded and ran back to Chet's booth. He was trembling. He let his breath out slowly. A narrow escape! Someone would surely have been hurt if the bonger had crashed.

Jay glanced about. Crowds were milling around the balloon man. Good! No one would have to know about the near tragedy.

"Hey!" called Tracy from her popcorn stand. "What was that all about? What happened?"

Jay called back, "I just wanted Sax and Chet to catch Marra's show."

Tracy chewed her gum thoughtfully. "I don't believe it," she said. "There's been another emergency."

Jay shook his head. He watched the balloon man walk toward the circle of rides, children following him. Jay looked at Colleen. She was busy with customers.

He frowned. What accident might happen next? How could the Spotlighters stop it when they didn't even know what it could be?

Jay's thoughts whirled. With so many people around, how could anyone have taken that big bolt out of the bonger without being seen? Or sawed through that support? How could—? Jay blinked. All these accidents had to be arranged at night. Loose parts, missing parts—whoever was doing it was doing it at night. Nothing was ever discovered until the next day. And then it was too late.

But how could anyone be here at night without being seen by the night watchman? What was his name, Hil? A night watchman would notice if—

Jay's thoughts were interrupted when Chet came back, swinging his toolkit. He waved to Jay. "Just a second, fella, I've got to see my Colleen."

Jay wondered whether Chet would tell her about the Big Bonger. Probably.

But would Colleen tell anyone else? Jay scratched his nose. As long as Kittles didn't find out, it wouldn't be too bad, he thought. Or Mr. McCoy.

Chet returned to his stand. "Thanks for keeping an eye on this for me."

"All fixed?" asked Jay.

"Better than ever," said Chet. "Say, it's lucky you noticed that missing bolt. It could have been a real disaster." Chet shook his head. "Sax has been pretty careless lately. He should inspect everything."

Jay started to say that it wasn't Sax's fault, but he stopped just in time. He didn't want anyone, except Sax himself, to know that the Spotlighters suspected all these things were being done on purpose.

"I hope nothing else goes wrong," said Jay.

"Nothing will now. Don't worry," answered Chet. He seemed to be in a good mood. "By the way, Sax told me to ask if you'd take tickets over at the Snake-a-roo. He's already got Dexter and Cindy at the other rides. Sax has lost all his records and everything's a mess. He just doesn't seem very well organized. It takes a lot of know-how to run a carnival."

Jay was silent.

"And Sax says you can leave when the ticket taker returns."

"We're getting a ride home," Jay said. "We can work later today. We really want this carnival to be a success."

"We all do," said Chet. "Keyhole Carnival, a permanent amusement park. I'll really like having—" He cut himself short. "Don't worry about the litter tonight. Hil always takes care of that."

58

Hil, the night watchman, thought Jay as he walked quickly over to the Snake-a-roo ride.

"Some carnival," grumbled the ticket taker as Jay came to take his place in the little booth. "It's payday and there's no pay."

"You'll get paid tomorrow," said Jay.

"Tomorrow ain't today," growled the ticket taker, walking off. "And I ain't the only one who's mad about it, either."

Jay frowned. The carnival was in trouble. He thought about it as he took tickets until the ticket taker returned. Then Jay went to find Cindy and Dexter.

"I'm starved," announced Dexter. "Let's talk about things over a dozen hot dogs. And that will just be the first dozen."

The three sat at one of the picnic tables in the circle of rides.

"Now I feel better," said Dexter, biting into a hot dog. Then he listened while Jay told about the near accident with the Big Bonger.

"I told Sax that someone was doing all of this on purpose," Jay said. "And he wouldn't believe me. He wouldn't listen."

"Well, he'll listen if we can find proof," said Cindy. She took out her notebook. "Let's put down everything we know."

She wrote in her notebook, *Suspects,* Kittles. *Motives,* Wants to make Keyhole Carnival look bad so he'll get his carnival chosen instead of Keyhole Carnival.

"Who besides Kittles has a motive?" she asked out loud.

"What about Tracy?" asked Dexter. "She used to work for Kittles. Maybe she's here spying or making trouble. Maybe she and Kittles are working together. Maybe he's told her if he gets his carnival in here permanently he'll give her a better job. Something like that."

"We're just guessing," objected Cindy.

"Put it down and then we can find out," suggested Jay. "Once we know what we're looking for, it's easier to find the facts."

Cindy wrote under *Suspects,* Tracy. Under *Motives* she wrote, Possibly a spy for Kittles.

"What about Chet?" asked Jay. "He's got a good motive. If Sax gets discouraged enough he'll sell Keyhole Carnival to Chet. And that's exactly

what Chet wants. He's said so to Colleen."

"Besides," added Dexter, "he's really a good mechanic. He can fix the machinery when it breaks down. But of course he can loosen parts of the machinery, too. He always seems to know just what's wrong."

Cindy sighed. "He may have a good motive, but that doesn't mean he is guilty. And—" She glanced at the boys. "Oh, all right, all right. I'm writing Chet down," she said.

She put Chet's name under *Suspects.* Under *Motives,* she wrote, So that Sax will get discouraged and sell out to Chet.

"And Colleen," said Dexter. "She could be doing it for Chet, knowing he wants to own the carnival. Or maybe they're doing it together."

Cindy frowned.

"Dex is right, Cindy," said Jay. "We have to suspect everybody. Writing Colleen's name down doesn't mean she's guilty. It just means we have to make sure that she's not."

Dexter nodded and leaned forward. "This is the only way we can solve the mystery. By suspecting everyone. Everyone who has a motive, that is."

Cindy nodded silently and wrote Colleen's name under *Suspects.*

She glanced at her notes. "There. I've written down all our suspects. Kittles. Tracy. Chet. Colleen. All the ones who have any motive."

"Any one of these suspects could have done these things at night," said Jay. "But what about the night watchman? Why wouldn't he see them?" He shook his head. "I started to think about that today, and then I got interrupted. Hil is here every night. Hil would see if anyone was prowling around." Jay hesitated, "Unless . . ."

Dexter finished the sentence, "Unless Hil is

doing all this, himself. What a perfect setup! How easy it would be!"

"But what's his motive?" asked Cindy.

"We'll have to find out," said Jay. "Let's see if he's here yet. Chet said Hil always comes at six."

The detectives looked around. "Which one is he?" whispered Cindy. She closed her notebook. "I'll ask Colleen," she decided. "See you in a second."

Cindy ran over to the souvenir booth. Colleen turned to her with a smile. "Guess what?" she asked, her eyes dancing. "Sax came over to talk to Chet. Just before the trouble with the Big Bonger. And Sax told Chet that if one more thing went wrong today, he'd sell out to Chet. Isn't that just wonderful?"

Cindy hesitated. "It isn't wonderful that things are going wrong," she said.

"I don't mean it that way," said Colleen quickly. "But don't you see? Things wouldn't be going wrong at all if Chet owned the carnival. Sax is very careless to let all these things happen."

A man with two kids walked toward the souvenir stand. Cindy spoke quickly. "Do you know where Hil, the night watchman, is?"

"Oh, sure," said Colleen. "Right over there at the tables. See?"

"Which one?" asked Cindy turning to look.

"The big one, in a gray sweat suit. Wiping off that table."

Cindy stared. "That woman?" asked Cindy. "Is that Hil? The night watchman?"

"You bet," said Colleen, turning to her customers.

Cindy ran back to the boys. "Hil's right over there. The big woman. In a gray sweat suit."

Dexter pushed his glasses down on his nose. "Well, let's go over and meet her," he said.

"Wait," said Cindy. "Colleen told me that if anything else goes wrong, Sax will sell out to Chet."

"Oh, no!" said Jay. "Sax doesn't want to sell. I guess all these accidents are making him lose confidence."

The Spotlighters walked quickly over to the table where Hil stood.

6 · Bewilderments

HIL'S LARGE BACK was to the Spotlighters as she wiped the table. Suddenly she turned. "Mercy!" she exclaimed. "You gave me a fright! And nobody scares Hil, nobody."

What a big woman, thought Cindy. She towered over the three detectives. Putting her large red hands on her hips, Hil looked down at them. Her squinty eyes must be the only small things about her, Cindy decided.

"When I got my mind going in one direction and something happens from t'other, I'm thrown clean off balance," said Hil. "Now I get a good look, and I see you're just three kids."

The Spotlighters smiled and told her about their new jobs at the carnival.

She tucked her thin brown hair under an old scarf. "I'm Hil, short for Hilda, not Hilary, as some might suspect. Awful glad to meet you folks," she added heartily.

She sat down hard on one of the benches. "Join me if you like, folks. Just got the table nice and clean for my spot of coffee."

The three detectives sat down with her at the table. Hil reached for a large red Thermos and poured herself a cup of steaming coffee. Then she looked around at the tables and down the lane between the two lines of stands.

"I got a job I'm mighty lucky to have," she said in her hearty voice. "The bright lights and people in the daytime. And then the quiet loneness of the night." She took a sip of her coffee. "I never sleep much. Can't find the use of it, to speak the truth."

"What do you do all night?" Jay asked.

"I make my rounds while I think thoughts," she said. "First up the left side of the keyhole, then around, then down the right side. Then up the middle, and all over again."

"I'd never be able to stay awake all night," Cindy said admiringly.

Hil looked at Cindy through her raisin eyes. "A kid like you needs sleep," she said. "I slept enough to last me a long time." She raised her Thermos cup to her lips and took a long swallow. She shook her head. "Coffee'll be the devil of me. That's a good cup of coffee, just like I always make. You wouldn't know it from my coffee last night—bitter tasting, it was." Then she gave a booming laugh. "Must be age creepin' up on me, folks. It can happen, and that's the plain truth."

The Spotlighters smiled. Hil took a final swallow of her coffee and then screwed the cup back on the Thermos. She rose from her chair, towering over the three detectives.

"I'll catch a spot of coffee with you later, if you're still around," she said. "Before I do my rounds I like to help close down a stand or two."

"We'll help, too," Dexter offered. "My sister won't be here to pick us up for a little while."

Hil's face lit up. "Why, you kids are real carnies," she boomed.

"Carnies?" Cindy asked. "What's that?"

"Why, carnies are carnival folk," Hil said. "A body working in a carnival is a carnie. All the good folks you see working here is one. Like me," she said proudly. "And now, of course, you folks, too."

Hil and the three Spotlighters helped lock up the stands and booths for the night.

"The plain truth is that it's getting dark," called Hil after a while. "And the plain truth of that is that now I start my night job."

She waved broadly to the three detectives and headed toward the rides, carrying her Thermos.

In a few minutes, the last of the carnies had left.

"Looks like we're the only ones here," Dexter said. "It's really quiet."

"Kind of spooky," said Jay.

"My big green pillow," said Cindy, remembering. "Now I can take it home since we're getting a ride. It's behind Colleen's stand."

The boys walked with Cindy back up the lane to Colleen's dark stand. Just as they were nearing it, Dexter stopped in his tracks.

"Look over there," he said, pointing toward the rides. "It looks like a fire!"

"Let's go," said Jay, breaking into a run.

The three detectives hurried toward the flickering light. They saw the large form of Hil kneeling on the ground. She was trying to set fire to something in a small cement incinerator. She muttered to herself and lighted another match.

"What's up, Hil?" asked Jay.

Hil dropped her box of matches on the ground and wheeled around. "Mercy!" she exclaimed. "You can't sneak up on Hil like that, folks. You got to give a bit of warning so her brain can catch up and not get jolted into tomorrow."

She heaved herself up and brushed her hands off on her sweat suit.

"Sorry, Hil," Cindy offered.

Hil grinned. "I'm having myself a devil of a time trying to light this fire. I like things neater than a pin. Can't stand having bits of paper and such lying unburned if they're meant to be burned."

"We'll help," Dexter volunteered, reaching down and picking up her box of matches.

"Why, you don't have to do such a thing. Kids shouldn't monkey with matches. I'll get the fire lit sooner or later—must be the dampness tonight."

Dexter peered down into the incinerator.

"We'll help," he said and lit a match. It flickered brightly over a sheaf of papers.

Suddenly he stared. The match burned down to his fingers, and he dropped it. "It's Sax's records!" he exclaimed. "And the payroll checks!"

Jay and Cindy ran to the incinerator and looked over Dexter's shoulder. Dexter reached down and picked up the papers. They were charred and half burned.

Hil's shadow loomed over the Spotlighters. "A bedevilment of all times!" she whispered, staring at the sheaf of papers in Dexter's hand.

"Somebody put them in here," Cindy said. "Whoever took them from Sax's house last night put them in here to burn." She turned to Hil. "Did you see anybody at all, Hil?" she asked. "Last night, maybe? Or tonight?"

Hil shook her head slowly. "Not a soul either night," she said.

"Whoever tried to destroy the papers probably thought they'd burn all the way," Dexter said. He turned to Hil. "We'll take these to Sax."

"Somebody took them from his trailer last night," said Jay. "There are some funny things that

70

have been going on around here, Hil. This is one of them."

Hil frowned. "Funny things?"

"Somebody is trying to hurt this carnival," explained Cindy. "Everything that's been done seems to have been done at night. So be careful, Hil."

Hil chuckled deeply. "If I'd been my parents, I'd have named me Careful," she said. "Don't you worry about Hil." She walked into the dark, away from them.

The Spotlighters hurried through the empty circle of rides to the trailer. A soft glow shone from the small windows. Dexter knocked on the door.

Sax opened the door quickly. "Oh," he said, his face falling. "I thought it was Marra. I don't know why, but she's gone off alone. Usually she waits for me. She says that on clear nights like this the stars all talk at once. It makes her head spin."

"Sax," Jay spoke up. "We have to talk to you. It's important."

"Important?" said Sax, frowning. "Well, do come in."

The Spotlighters followed him into the small,

overcrowded living room. He turned to face them. "What's wrong?"

"We have to tell you something," said Dexter. He thrust the half-burned papers toward Sax. "Your missing records. The checks you were going to sign. Someone did take them—and tried to burn them."

Sax reached out for the charred papers. He looked at them as if he didn't understand what they were. Then he looked up. "But who took them? Who did this?" he asked.

The Spotlighters hesitated. "We're detectives," said Dexter.

"Detectives? You kids?" Sax shook his head. "Everything's all mixed up. You mean that you've found out something? Something I don't know?"

"We're trying to find out," said Jay. "We can't accuse anyone until we know for sure. Otherwise we might accuse an innocent person. That wouldn't be fair."

Cindy thought quickly. That would have to be one of their rules. A Fair Rule. Not to discuss their suspicions with anyone until they had proof.

Sax looked from one to the other. "Thank you

for coming. Thank you for trying to help. But now I must find Marra. Will you do me a favor?" He walked quickly to the table and picked up an envelope. "I just made out another check to Hil. She needs it tonight. Would you please take this to her?"

"Of course," Cindy said, taking the envelope.

"But, Sax," Jay said. "You do believe us, don't you? Someone is trying to make you give up your carnival."

Sax hesitated. Then he said, "Everything will be all right. But I have to find Marra. She must have gone to her sister's. She often does that. Please excuse me." And he slipped out of the trailer door and in a moment was out of sight in the dark.

"Poor Sax!" whispered Cindy. "He's worried about the carnival, and he's worried about Marra."

"He just doesn't want to believe anyone would want to hurt him," said Jay.

The Spotlighters were quiet a moment.

"Let's find Hil," suggested Dexter. "We have to give her the pay envelope."

They left the trailer and walked through the darkness toward the rides.

"Hil!" Jay called. There was no answer.

"She could be checking the rides," said Cindy. "You take the caterpillar and I'll take the merry-go-round." It was so dim that Cindy could barely see her way. "Hil!" she called. There was no reply.

Ahead, Cindy could make out the shadowy outline of the horses on the merry-go-round. Suddenly she stared. Something had caught her eye, just for a second. Something shining. She hurried forward. Was it inside the merry-go-round? She stepped up on the platform and looked around. There it was again—a movement of something shining. She leaned forward. Something round was swinging gently from a broken chain. It was caught on the machinery that operated the merry-go-round. It was shining and swinging and turning. A medallion or a locket, Cindy thought, one with a design.

As she stared at it, Cindy was suddenly aware of something else. Someone was sitting on one of the benches between the horses. A dark, silent shape.

"Hil?" Cindy said softly. There was no answer. "Hil?" Cindy said again. Silence. Cindy's heart thudded. If it was Hil, she'd answer me, she thought. And if it wasn't Hil, then who was it? And then the dark form shifted and fell down on the bench, motionless.

Cindy screamed. Then there were running footsteps.

"Cindy?" It was Jay. "Where are you? What's happened?"

"There's someone—" Cindy tried to say. The two boys rushed up to her, and she pointed to the still figure on the bench. They stared.

"I thought it was Hil, but she didn't answer and then suddenly—" Cindy was interrupted by a deep groan.

"It *is* Hil," Dexter said, bending over the still form.

"Hil!" Cindy cried, her throat dry.

"You okay, Hil?" Dexter asked nervously. He reached down to touch the big woman's shoulder.

Hil pulled herself up slowly to a sitting position. She shook her head. "Where am I?" she said thickly. "What's happening?"

"We came to look for you," Jay said. "You didn't answer when we called."

Hil rubbed her face with her large hands. She spoke in a slurred mumble. They leaned closer to hear her.

"I don't know what's what, and that's the truth," she said. She shook her head again, harder. "I can't get my mind to catch up with me," she mumbled. "Like I'm awake and it's asleep." She nodded, and her head fell to one side.

"She's going back to sleep," said Cindy, shaking her. "Hil!" she said. "Stay awake! Please!"

The big woman nodded. "Awake," she said. "Coffee keeps me awake. But this time—"Her voice trailed off.

"Are you sick?" asked Dexter. The Spotlighters looked at Hil with concern.

"Woozy," Hil said thickly. "I sat here a spell with my coffee. And then—and then I just blacked out. Never happened before." She rubbed her hands over her face once more. "Never before last night. It happened last night, too."

Jay's heart pounded faster. Hil had said that her coffee tasted bitter last night. It hadn't tasted like her own regular coffee.

"How did your coffee taste tonight?" Jay asked.

Hil shook her head, trying to stay awake. "Fine when I was with you kids. Then bitter, but I finished it anyway. It didn't keep me awake. It—"

"A sleeping pill!" gasped Cindy. "Someone must have put it in your Thermos!"

"I don't understand," mumbled Hil. "No one would do that to Hil."

Dexter leaned forward. "Remember we told you that strange things had been going on around here?"

Hil nodded slowly.

"Well, someone's been trying to ruin the carnival. Whoever it is wanted you asleep so you wouldn't see or hear anything. Someone gave you a sleeping pill."

Hil sat up straighter. "Why, that is out and out mean," she said. Her voice was stronger now. "Who would do such a thing to Hil?"

She started to lift herself off the bench and sat down hard. "A mite woozy yet. A bit of to and fro and I'll be as good as new."

"We'll walk you up and down and then take you over to Sax's trailer," said Jay.

The Spotlighters helped Hil off the merry-go-round. With Jay on one side and Dexter on the other, they walked with her until she felt stronger.

"I don't like that," Hil kept saying. "To think someone would do that to Hil. I don't get mad easy, folks, but when I do, I'm really mad."

The four headed for Sax's trailer. They knocked, but there was no answer.

"Sax must still be looking for Marra," Cindy said. "He wouldn't mind if we brought Hil in," she added, pushing open the door. The Spotlighters helped Hil to the couch.

"Mighty glad you folks came around again," Hil said, color returning to her round cheeks. "I might've slept into tomorrow for all I know."

"Oh," Cindy said, reaching into her pocket. "I forgot your check with everything that happened. Sax asked us to give you your check—he wrote out a new one."

"Well, now," Hil said, smiling broadly. "If that Sax isn't the biggest lump of humanity." She reached for the check and tucked it away.

Suddenly Cindy turned to the boys. "I saw something there at the merry-go-round," she said excitedly. "I forgot all about it till just now. It was like a silver medal or locket or something, hanging from a chain. Something you'd wear around your neck, maybe. It was just hanging there from one of the gears. As if it was caught."

"Someone must have been doing something to the gears," Jay guessed.

"To mess up the merry-go-round!" Dexter said.

"Let's go check!" the boys said at once.

"I'll stay with Hil," Cindy said. "Hurry back. And be careful."

As Cindy was bringing a tall glass of water to Hil, the boys returned and burst through the door.

"It's not there!" Jay said. "We looked everywhere. Are you sure you saw something, Cindy?"

"Positive," she answered.

"Then somebody came and took it away while we were here with Hil," Dexter said slowly. "He must have missed it when he got home and decided to come back for it. Whoever lost it knew it would identify him if it was found."

"I'm going to leave a note for Sax," Cindy said, tearing a page out of her notebook. "To tell him to check the merry-go-round first thing in the morning." She wrote busily and put the note where she was sure Sax would see it.

"Bewilderments and bedevilments on top of each other!" exclaimed Hil.

"You can come home with us," Dexter offered. "My sister is picking us up. Then you won't have to—"

"And miss the chance of more excitement?" she

asked, her small eyes shining. "Not a chance! I'm feeling just like my old strong self. I just won't drink any more coffee, and that's the plain truth."

She heaved herself up off the couch. "And now back to work," she said firmly. "You kids run on home."

"But—" Cindy started to say.

"Scat!" Hil boomed.

The Spotlighters looked at each other.

"No use trying to convince me otherwise, folks," Hil said, pushing them out the door. "You get home quick like. Now." She stood looking at them for a second in the dark with her hands on her large hips. Then she turned and headed toward the rides.

The three detectives hurried to the entrance, where Anne's car would be.

"Let's pick up your green pillow," suggested Jay, heading for Colleen's stand.

Somehow the pillow didn't seem very important to Cindy now. She looked over her shoulder. Someone had drugged Hil's coffee so she'd fall asleep and not hear or see anything. Kittles? Tracy? Chet? Colleen? Who did it? And what about the silver locket or whatever it was Cindy had seen? To whom did it belong?

Anne and Mike, her date, were waiting for the three detectives. "What took you so long?" Anne demanded. "Another mystery, I'll bet. And I'll bet it has something to do with that green pillow." She laughed, and so did Mike.

The Spotlighters were silent on the way home, their thoughts whirling. There was danger at Keyhole Carnival.

7 · *The Picture Is Dark*

CHILDREN'S VOICES woke Cindy the next morning. Amy and Randy were playing outside her window. She heard them through her dreams.

She had been dreaming of carnival lights going around and around. Around and around and flashing on and off. Flashing danger. And the round silver disc turning slowly, slowly, on its broken chain.

She heard Amy's voice. "I can tell time longer than you can!"

"Can't," Randy said back.

Cindy rubbed her eyes and sat up in bed. What time was it, anyway? She looked at her watch on the night stand next to her bed. Late.

She kept looking at her watch. What had she just been dreaming?

"Look, Randy," Amy's voice shouted. "I'm a clock."

"Your arms are too short," laughed Randy.

At once Cindy was wide awake. The silver disc. It wasn't a medallion after all. It was a pocket watch. A watch with a cover that snapped open to show the face. A "peek" watch.

Cindy sprang out of bed. She threw on her clothes and raced down the stairs. Amy and Randy were playing tag on the Temples' front lawn.

"Hi, Cindy," Randy called, running up to her. Amy trotted behind him.

"Remember yesterday at the carnival?" asked Cindy.

"Balloons!" cried Amy.

"Remember when a man took your picture?"

"Yes, yes, yes," said Amy. "He had things hanging from his coat, boxes."

"Those were cameras, Amy," said Randy.

"Do you remember the man who showed you the funny watch? A man who had his picture taken with you?" Cindy asked, looking at Randy.

Randy frowned. "Well, maybe sort of," he said. "Was he the man with the balloons?"

Cindy closed her eyes. "I don't know, Randy. I'm asking you. Was he tall? Short?"

"He was taller than me," Randy said positively. "But maybe it wasn't the balloon man. No. It wasn't. The balloon man wouldn't let go of his balloons."

"He gave me one, but it went bang!" said Amy, hopping up and down.

"Not that man, Amy," Randy said. He frowned again. "Maybe it was—no, it couldn't have been. We got our picture taken an awful lot," he added, looking worried.

Cindy sighed. "Don't worry, Randy. Thanks, kids." She turned and hurried back in the house.

She ran up to Jay's room. He was still asleep. "It was a watch!" she said, shaking Jay's shoulder. "The watch that someone showed to Amy and Randy yesterday at the carnival!"

"What?" asked Jay. He sat up in bed. "Wait! I can't think until I open my eyes. Now say that again, slowly."

Cindy took a deep breath. "Yesterday at the carnival. Skip Bannerman took a picture of Amy and Randy with someone who had a round silver watch. A watch with a cover that opened to show the face. That's what I saw last night on the merry-go-round. I'm sure of it. A watch, not a medallion or locket."

Suddenly Jay sprang into action. "Let's ask Amy and Randy," he said.

"I did. They don't remember," said Cindy. "We've got to ask Skip Bannerman. He's coming back to the carnival today to take more pictures."

"I'll call Dex, while you're getting dressed," said Cindy.

It was ten o'clock when the three detectives passed McCoy's Warehouse and arrived at Keyhole Carnival. Jay and Cindy had their own bikes, but Dexter had borrowed Anne's old one.

An old car pulled in behind them. A young man with long dark hair was at the wheel. Two people sat beside him. Cindy blinked. It was Sax and Marra.

They got out of the car, and Marra leaned into the window to say good-bye to the driver. "Your baby is the most beautiful new baby in the whole world! I knew it would come last night. It's like a little bird."

As they came to the entrance of Keyhole Carnival, Sax and Marra saw the Spotlighters. Marra called, "Guess what we've seen? A brand new, tiny baby, and I'm an aunt. My sister's baby was born last night." Her face shone with happiness.

Jay spoke quickly to Sax. "Did you find the note I left last night?"

Sax shook his head, puzzled. "What note?"

"In the trailer," said Jay.

"I didn't get back to the trailer after I saw you," explained Sax. "I went to the house where Marra's sister and her husband live. I thought that's where Marra had gone—she knew their baby would be born soon."

Sax paused and frowned. "But you weren't at your sister's house when I got there, Marra."

"I was dancing under the stars, thinking of names for the baby," said Marra softly.

Cindy glanced over at Marra. Her silver rings and bracelets and chains around her neck caught the morning sun.

"Anyway," Marra laughed, "I came in time to see the new baby. And her name is Star. Isn't that lovely?"

For a moment everyone just smiled at everyone else. Then Dexter pushed his glasses up on his forehead and said, "Sax, we left a note last night telling you that we think you'll find something wrong with the merry-go-round this morning."

"The merry-go-round?" Sax asked, no longer smiling. He turned to Marra. He started to say, "Marra, you," but broke into a run. Jay, Cindy, and Dexter followed as he headed toward the merry-go-round.

"Oh, the poor merry-go-round," Marra called as she danced along, trying to keep up with the others.

Cindy's eyes darted anxiously around. The carnival was just stirring. The booths were being readied for the day. Chet was opening his.

"Grab your toolbox, Chet," Sax called urgently. "We've got to fix the merry-go-round."

Chet stared. "But how do you know anything's wrong?" he asked, frowning. "The operator isn't due until noon."

"Hurry," urged Sax. "We've got to have it running before we open the carnival."

Still frowning, Chet reached for his toolbox.

Sax turned to Jay and Dexter. "Since I'll be tied up with Chet working on the merry-go-round, could you kids do me a big favor? As long as you're here early, would you mind unpacking the new shipment of prizes? Tracy can help the three of you. She knows which prizes go to which booth, and how many and so on."

"We'll be glad to, Sax," said Dexter.

"Just ask Tracy," said Sax. Then he hurried to the merry-go-round. Marra followed him.

The Spotlighters found Tracy and told her they would help unpack the new shipment of prizes.

"Well, that's a relief," said Tracy. "I thought I'd be stuck with the whole job." She shook her head. "When I worked for Kittles, he hired someone just to take care of the shipments of prizes. Here at Keyhole Carnival, everybody overlaps, everybody has to pitch in."

"I like it this way," said Cindy. "It's fun to do different jobs."

"Yeah, you learn more," said Jay.

Tracy sniffed. "You work harder, that's all," she said.

Tracy explained what to do. They all worked,

unpacking the boxes of prizes and carrying them to the booths.

Cindy kept glancing up to see if Skip Bannerman was coming. She couldn't wait to ask him whom he'd photographed with a silver pocket watch. With Amy and Randy. The Spotlighters were so close to solving their mystery!

Cindy finished unpacking one of the boxes. Then she looked at her watch. It was eleven thirty. The carnival would open at twelve. She wondered whether Chet and Sax had repaired the merry-go-round. She decided to find out.

They were still working. Sax straightened up. "There," he said with a sigh of relief. "It's okay now." He looked around. "Has the carnival opened yet? What time is it?"

Cindy started to say that it was eleven forty-five, but she held her breath. Chet was putting his tools away.

"Chet, is it noon yet?" asked Sax.

Cindy stared at Chet. Would he pull out a pocket watch? A round silver pocket watch with a cover over its face?

Chet kept his head down, closing his toolbox.

"I don't know," he said. "I don't have my watch with me." He stood up, stretched, and went on, "I'll go on back to my stand, Sax. I've got to get it opened."

"Thanks for helping. I don't know what I'd do without you, Chet. You're a great mechanic. You always know exactly what's gone wrong." Sax smiled. "It's almost as if you have ESP, like Marra."

Chet turned and started to walk back to his booth. "Oh, it's just a sixth sense that good mechanics have," he said.

"I hope that things go smoothly today," worried Sax. "I'm so shorthanded already. Kittles has hired two more of my people away from me. I couldn't schedule an operator for the Tilt-a-whirl until two o'clock today. And I can only open it by closing the Snapdragon."

"I know," said Chet over his shoulder. "You told me yesterday."

"Well, things will be better today," said Sax. "If not, what I said still goes. I'll have to sell."

Chet stopped in his tracks. Then he turned back to Sax with a smile. "That's a deal," he said and walked on.

"Don't worry, Sax," said Cindy, wanting to help some way.

Sax shook his head. "I don't want to worry, but everything seems to be going wrong. Maybe Marra is right. I should sell out. I've got to talk to her." He walked quickly to his trailer.

Cindy was thoughtful as she returned to the line of booths. It was almost twelve o'clock. The crowds were just starting to trickle in. Suddenly she spotted Skip Bannerman with his cameras slung over his shoulders.

Cindy ran over to him. "I'm so glad you're here," she said, out of breath.

"Well, that's nice," said Skip, smiling at her. "I like to be popular."

"Skip, do you remember yesterday you took a picture of two kids talking to someone with a watch?"

Skip pulled his ear. "Two kids and someone with a watch?"

Cindy nodded eagerly.

"Well, now, young lady, let me ask you a question. Do you know how many kids were here yesterday? And how many people with or without watches? Do you have any idea how many pictures I took?" He pulled his ear again. "I want you to know that the chances of my remembering any particular picture are about one in six million. Now, have I answered your question?"

"Two little kids," repeated Cindy. "A boy and a girl, and someone with a watch that—"

Skip shook his head firmly.

"Oh, you've got to remember," begged Cindy. "You've got to!"

"And you have to remember that I am only human, not a computer," said Skip Bannerman. "If I could remember details like that, I'd be on one of those TV shows. 'Mystery Brain Remembers All, Stuns Scientists,' I can see it in print. Sorry, I wish I could help you if it makes all that difference." He paused. "I'll tell you what you could try. I took lots of pictures. Some of them will be used in the paper, and some won't. I don't know which ones have been chosen for today's paper. But maybe the picture you're looking for is one of them—if you're lucky."

"Today's paper?" asked Cindy.

He nodded. "It will be out this afternoon."

"Thanks!" called Cindy as she hurried off to

find Jay and Dexter. They were nowhere in sight. Finally she found them carrying empty boxes to put behind Sax's trailer.

"I found Skip Bannerman," she whispered.

"You don't need to whisper," said Jay. "Sax and Marra have left. He's going to run the Ferris wheel, and she's going to take a ride on the merry-go-round. What's up?"

Cindy explained, "Skip doesn't remember the silver watch. But the picture we want just might be in this afternoon's paper. We can pick up a copy after two o'clock at Colleen's stand. Of course, the picture may not be in the paper. But it's worth a try."

Dexter broke in. "While we were working on the boxes of prizes, Kittles came," he said. "And guess what? Tracy told him all about the merry-go-round breaking down."

"That Tracy!" said Cindy angrily. "Whose side is she on, anyway?"

Jay grinned. "That's just what Colleen asked her when she heard about it. And Tracy said she was on whichever side was going to win. We didn't hear all that. Colleen told us. She was really burned up at Tracy for telling Kittles about the merry-go-round."

"By the way, Cindy," said Dexter. "Sax wants to see you at the Ferris wheel."

Cindy nodded and went to find Sax. He was running the Ferris wheel, stopping it from time to

time to let riders on and off. He looked over at Cindy and smiled.

"You wanted to see me, Sax?" she asked.

He nodded. "Marra's riding the merry-go-round," he said.

Cindy looked at Sax. He was tired and worried. And no wonder, she thought.

"I wonder if you'd just keep her company for a little while," said Sax softly. "I'm so busy, I'm afraid she's lonely. You understand?"

Cindy nodded quickly as Sax went on. "Mr. McCoy is on his way to see me. In fact, here he comes now. He wants to talk. When Marra is tired of the merry-go-round, perhaps you could take another ride with her, something like that."

"I'd love to," said Cindy. Now she really understood. Sax wanted Marra kept busy while Mr. McCoy was there.

At that moment Mr. McCoy walked over to Sax. He stretched out his hand. Sax smiled and they shook hands. Then Mr. McCoy said, "I just wanted to have a little visit, Sax. I like your carnival. I like it very much. I like the spirit, the flavor, the friendliness."

"Thank you, Mr. McCoy," said Sax.

The older man paused. "I am a little worried, however. I realize that this man Kittles is a tattle-tale and a troublemaker. But I've been doing some checking, on my own of course, and I've heard a few disturbing stories."

Cindy held her breath.

Mr. McCoy continued, "I like this carnival, as I say. I would like it to remain here in Kenoska as a permanent carnival, part of a regular amusement park. But I cannot recommend a carnival which has repeated mishaps."

Sax shook his head despairingly. "Don't judge my carnival by what's been happening lately, Mr. McCoy. This is just a lot of bad luck. Nothing else will happen, I know." He glanced at Cindy.

Mr. McCoy nodded. "For all our sakes, I hope that nothing else happens. I've tried to give you every chance, every benefit of the doubt. But if anything else goes wrong, you understand, I will be forced to report to the committee this afternoon that Keyhole Carnival is not safe."

Cindy gulped.

Then Mr. McCoy lowered his voice. "Frankly,

I would not be able to recommend the carnival Kittles runs. 'A man of no principle, I'm afraid. It's your carnival or none at all." He straightened his tie.

Cindy glanced at Sax. He said quietly, "I understand, Mr. McCoy."

Mr. McCoy turned to go. "I have a board meeting now, and my warehouse needs some attention, too. But I'll be back later this afternoon before I complete my report on the carnival." He smiled and reached for Sax's hand. Then he left, walking past the booths and toward the Keyhole Carnival exit.

Sax fingered one of his bracelets. "Nothing more will happen today," he said. "Nothing must." He looked at Cindy. "And you'll be with Marra, won't you? She's been worried. You can take her mind off everything—I hate to have her worried."

Cindy nodded. "I'm on my way to the merry-go-round right now," she said. "Don't worry about Marra."

8 · Up in the Air

CINDY REACHED the merry-go-round quickly. The horse that Marra rode was on the outside edge. Cindy walked closer. Marra saw her and waved. Each time the horse came around, Marra blew a kiss.

Cindy couldn't help smiling. Marra was a lot like a little girl. A little girl who didn't want to grow up, who didn't want to worry. Cindy felt years and years older than Marra. "And maybe I am," she thought. "I've aged ten years this week, worrying."

Finally the merry-go-round slowed and stopped. Marra hopped off her horse. Cindy ran around to meet her. Marra's eyes were shining.

"Oh, don't you love merry-go-rounds?" asked Marra. "Up and down and around, all at once. Things look so blurry. And then when you stop, everything looks so clear again." She smiled wistfully. "I like the blurry better than the clear, don't you?" she asked.

Cindy smiled back. "I don't mind the clear at all," she said.

Marra laughed and held out her hand. "Let's do a ride together, shall we? I hate the noisy ones that jerk you around. I know—let's go on the Ferris wheel!" she said, pulling Cindy along with her.

Skip Bannerman was standing with his camera at the Ferris wheel, talking to Sax. "I'd like some real human interest pictures of you, Sax," Skip said.

Marra interrupted breathlessly. "Sax, we want to ride on the Ferris wheel. We want to go up to the sky itself!"

"I'd like to get your picture, Mrs. Darby," Skip said. "Standing next to your husband. 'Carnival Couple Makes Good, Better, Best.' How's that for a picture title?"

Marra gave him a dazzling smile. "I like that, Skipper, I like that. You give me good vibes."

Skip took a picture of Sax and Marra, standing together smiling. "And now, if I may, I'd like to take a picture of the two of you in a Ferris wheel car. 'Carnival Owners on Way Up.' "

Marra laughed lightly. "On the way up, Sax," she said. She climbed into the car of the Ferris wheel. Sax hesitated, then joined her.

Skip Bannerman took the picture.

"And now it's the girl's turn to get in with me," said Marra. "And you run the thing, won't you?" she said to Sax. "I only feel safe when you're in charge."

Marra and Cindy climbed into the car. "We'll go up, up, up to where the clouds live and bump and gather together for tea," Marra called.

Skip muttered as he wrote in his notebook, " 'Carnival Wife Lives in Clouds.' "

Cindy and Marra rose, their car gently swaying.

As they began to climb, Cindy saw with a start that Kittles seemed to be arguing with the operator of the Tilt-a-whirl. She wished she was not on the Ferris wheel so that she could find out what he was saying.

She looked around for Jay and Dexter, but couldn't see them anywhere. Maybe they were buying a newspaper, she thought. And maybe in the paper would be a picture of someone showing a watch to Amy and Randy, a round silver watch.

And then Cindy saw that the Tilt-a-whirl had started up. A long line of children were waiting for their turns. Laughter from below carried up to Cindy. Up that high, she felt she could see and hear everything.

She glanced down and saw Skip Bannerman with all his cameras walking toward the Tilt-a-whirl.

"Don't you just love floating and rocking?" Marra exclaimed. Cindy smiled and looked over Marra's shoulder at the other side of the carnival. Mr. McCoy was walking from a car to his warehouse, just beyond the park grounds.

Suddenly the laughter Cindy had heard from the children at the Tilt-a-whirl changed to crying. She looked down. The Tilt-a-whirl was stopped and children were unable to get out of the cars.

What had happened to the Tilt-a-whirl? Crowds were gathering. There were angry shouts.

What had Sax said about the Tilt-a-whirl? That he couldn't open it until after two o'clock because he was so shorthanded. Cindy glanced at her watch. Just after two. Had the ride been tampered with last night? It looked that way.

Cindy closed her eyes. Why hadn't anyone thought about inspecting the Tilt-a-whirl? Sax should have checked all the rides before he opened them today. But of course he and Chet had been busy repairing the merry-go-round.

Cindy opened her eyes and leaned forward to look around. She and Marra were still several cars from the ground. Then she inwardly groaned when she saw Kittles gesturing to Skip Bannerman and leading him to the Tilt-a-whirl. Now Skip would take pictures of crying children on a broken ride.

She prayed that Mr. McCoy would stay in his warehouse and not come and see this new disaster. He'd say the carnival was not safe, that it would have to be closed. And then Sax would never be able to have a permanent carnival in Kenoska.

"Please hurry, Ferris wheel," Cindy said to herself. She had to get off and reach Skip to ask him not to take those pictures.

"Oh, that bad Sax!" said Marra. "He's bringing us down again. I want to stay up here forever."

Cindy hardly listened to Marra. What was happening at the Tilt-a-whirl? And where were Jay and Dexter?

When the car reached the bottom, Cindy jumped out as soon as Sax raised the safety bar.

"Would you like to come over for soup?" Marra asked her.

"Maybe later," Cindy said hastily. She ran quickly to the Tilt-a-whirl.

Children were sitting in the stalled cars, unable to step out. Angry cries and confused wailing met Cindy's cars as she stared at the Tilt-a-whirl.

"Some carnival!" Cindy heard a disgruntled man say. "Nothing works. Let's get out of here."

Cindy looked for Skip and then heard his voice. "'Broken Ride Means Broken Hearts,'" he muttered. She spun around. "'End of Ride Means End of Dream,'" he said.

"Skip!" Cindy cried. "Please, you can't do that! You were taking such happy pictures before and—"

"News happens fast. In a flash the picture changes," Skip told her, reloading his camera.

"Since our last meeting, I have had my ears bent in another direction. I have learned from a very reliable source that all manner of things have been going wrong with Keyhole Carnival. This is one example. My source gave me others. I believe, in fact, that you and your friends have kindly steered me away from other disasters. I'm just catching up

with what's really going on, thanks to a public-spirited man named Kittles. He doesn't like to see a carelessly run carnival."

"But that isn't fair!" cried Cindy.

"All's fair in newsgathering," Skip answered. "Look at these disappointed kids. I've already taken pictures of four of them. One snuffling, one bawling, one pouting, one kicking at his mother. Perfect."

"But why don't you go to another ride where there are happy faces?" asked Cindy.

"I've done that already this week. But that isn't really news, is it? Bad news sells more papers than good news does. And this is bad news, honey, and I'm going to make the best of it. Or the worst of it. 'Carnival Breathes Its Last.'" Then seeing Cindy's face, he added, "Hey, look. I'm sorry, but this is my job," and his camera flashed and flashed again.

Cindy's eyes stung. If she hadn't gone on that long ride with Marra this wouldn't have happened. She'd have been able to steer Skip away from the Tilt-a-whirl.

Cindy clenched her fists. "It isn't fair," she said again. But it was no use. Skip Bannerman was already interviewing a pair of angry parents.

It *wasn't* fair. Sax's Carnival was going to be held up to ridicule. Sax wouldn't have a chance. And it wasn't his fault. It wasn't his fault at all!

Cindy took a deep breath. She couldn't stop Skip Bannerman—it was too late for that. She would have to get to Mr. McCoy. He could help. He'd been fair all along, bending over backward to give Sax the benefit of the doubt when all these things began to happen.

She could go to him. She could tell Mr. McCoy that the accidents hadn't been accidents at all. They were all part of a plan, a mean plan to keep Keyhole Carnival from staying in Kenoska. Tears stung her eyes. She could do something to help, she *could*.

Cindy straightened her shoulders. From the top of the Ferris wheel she had seen Mr. McCoy getting out of a car at his warehouse. She'd go to him and say it wasn't Sax's fault at all. There was an enemy. She didn't know who it was yet, but there was an enemy.

Cindy turned and ran toward the warehouse.

9 · Closing In

CINDY WAS OUT OF BREATH by the time she reached the warehouse. She pushed against the door and pounded.

Half sobbing, Cindy pounded again. And suddenly the door opened, and she half fell into the brightly lighted warehouse.

"Well, well, what's this? What's wrong?" asked Mr. McCoy, frowning in surprise.

"Mr. McCoy, I have to talk to you," gulped Cindy.

"Well, you are," said Mr. McCoy. "But do step

in." He turned and spoke to a man leaning against some crates, drinking a Coke.

"Stan, why don't you finish your Coke outside?" he asked. The man sauntered out the door.

Mr. McCoy turned back to Cindy. "Now. Just relax. Tell me all about it. Is anything wrong?"

"Everything," said Cindy, catching her breath. "The things going wrong at Keyhole Carnival. The accidents. They're not accidents. Someone's trying to wreck Sax's carnival. And now Skip Bannerman is taking pictures of all the bad things instead of all the good things, it will all be in the paper, and—"

"Now slow down, young lady," Mr. McCoy said kindly.

Cindy was afraid she was going to cry. She swallowed three times, fast. That was her usual trick to keep from crying. She hoped it would work. It always had before.

"The things that have been happening aren't accidents, Mr. McCoy. Someone is arranging them." She took a new breath.

Mr. McCoy pushed his lip out. "Have you proof of this, this strange idea? Do you know who has been doing these things?"

"We have proof that these things were done on purpose," Cindy said. "But we don't have proof about who it *is*. Yet. But we will."

"I see," Mr. McCoy said, frowning. "You're just guessing."

"Mr. McCoy, you've got to help," Cindy said. "You've got to. We may not have any proof yet, but we will."

"But young lady, what can I do? How can I help?" asked Mr. McCoy.

"You have a lot of influence. And you've been fair to Sax. You've given him an extra chance. I want you to come and talk to Skip Bannerman. Talk him out of a story in his newspaper that will be against Keyhole Carnival. You can do it, Mr. McCoy, I know you can, and you're the only one who can help." She swallowed three times quickly.

"Let me get this straight," said Mr. McCoy. "Someone is really trying to make the carnival look bad? Trying to cause accidents? It isn't just poor management?"

Cindy nodded.

Mr. McCoy rubbed his finger over his lip. "This is a very serious charge. I need to know the facts before I can help."

"Chet's stand collapsed because one of the supports was sawed through," said Cindy. "And—oh, Mr. McCoy, there's so much to tell you! It will be too late for you to help if I try to tell you everything now. Please come over to the carnival. Please get Skip Bannerman to stop taking pictures of the bad things. Please."

Mr. McCoy rubbed his chin. He walked over to a desk that was in a little office. Then he turned to Cindy. "I know you're serious. I know you believe what you are saying. But these are things that must be examined." He reached into his pocket.

"Let's say that I meet you over there in fifteen minutes. Is that all right?"

He took out of his pocket a round silver watch. It had a design on the cover. Cindy stared. The watch was on a broken chain. Mr. McCoy pressed a button on the side of the watch, and a lid sprang open.

Cindy bit her tongue. Not to keep from crying this time. To keep from screaming. This was the watch she had seen swinging back and forth on the merry-go-round.

"Let's say, then," Mr. McCoy said, "that I meet you at two-thirty."

"At two-thirty," repeated Cindy, her heart pounding as she stared at the silver watch. The watch she had seen while Hil slept. And Hil had slept because someone had put a sleeping pill in her coffee. That person was Mr. McCoy!

Cindy thought fast. "I'll be at the Ferris wheel,

if that's all right, Mr. McCoy. I'll ask Skip Bannerman to meet us there. He might want to take a picture of you and happy kids on the Ferris wheel."

Mr. McCoy snapped his silver pocket watch shut. He nodded. "At two-thirty, then. We'll get to the bottom of this, don't you worry. Meantime, I'll be glad to help this Skip Bannerman take some cheerful pictures."

"I'm so glad you'll help us," said Cindy. As she walked to the door she kept telling herself, "Move slowly, slowly." She did not look back when she slowly opened the door. "I've got to pretend I haven't noticed anything, I've got to pretend I haven't noticed anything," she repeated over and over to herself.

She forced herself to walk, not run, across the empty lot. It's been Mr. McCoy all along, she thought. The real McCoy. But why did he want Keyhole Carnival to fail? Why had he drugged Hil? He must have fixed the merry-go-round so that it wouldn't go, and the Tilt-a-whirl, too. But why? Her mind spun.

When she was sure she was out of Mr. McCoy's sight, she broke into a run.

It took only three minutes to find the boys, but to Cindy it felt like three years. Jay and Dexter were walking along hurriedly, looking in every direction.

"It's Mr. McCoy!" she said in a whisper. "It's been Mr. McCoy all along."

"We know," Jay said quickly. "We just found out. Look at this. We've been looking all over for you."

He thrust a newspaper under Cindy's nose. She blinked and looked at it. Jay pointed. It was a picture of Amy and Randy Maxwell. A man next to them was showing them a watch. The man was Mr. McCoy.

Cindy stared at the picture and then at Jay and Dexter.

"How did *you* find out?" Dexter asked. "Did you see the newspaper, too?"

Cindy shook her head. "I wanted to help Sax some way. I wanted to keep Skip Bannerman from turning in an awful story about all the things wrong at Keyhole Carnival. Mr. McCoy was the only person I could think of who could help. So I went over to his warehouse—that's when I saw his silver watch. It springs open when he presses the stem.

Amy's peek watch," finished Cindy, trying to smile.

Then she spoke quickly. "He's coming over to meet me in a few minutes. At the Ferris wheel. I told him I'd try to get Skip Bannerman there to take pictures. We've got to think of some way to trap him. We know he's guilty, but we have no proof. No one will believe us."

The Spotlighters stared helplessly at each other.

"He *must* have a motive," Dexter said. "Nobody would be doing all this without a reason."

"A motive, a motive," Jay muttered. "Why doesn't he want this carnival here?"

"His warehouse," Cindy said slowly. "It's right near the carnival. Maybe there's something in his warehouse he doesn't want anybody to know about. If there was a permanent amusement park here, there would be a chance of someone stumbling onto something."

"Like stolen goods!" guessed Dexter. Suddenly he snapped his fingers. "I have an idea. Cindy, make sure Sax is running the Ferris wheel. Jay, find Skip and get him to the Ferris wheel in a hurry—tell him it'll be a good picture."

Then Dexter pulled Jay and Cindy to one side and spoke quickly, explaining his idea. Jay and Cindy smiled.

At 2:30 Mr. McCoy appeared at the foot of the Ferris wheel. Cindy was there with Sax. The boys stood a little distance away. Cindy could barely look at Mr. McCoy. She was afraid her feelings would show on her face.

Skip Bannerman came up, and he and Mr. McCoy shook hands. Skip saw Cindy and winked cheerfully.

"I understand that there's been a slight mishap with another ride," Mr. McCoy said to Skip Bannerman.

Cindy felt Sax stiffen beside her.

"But let's not make such a mountain out of it," he went on. "As long as you have a story to write, why not make it a happy one?" He smiled. "Pictures of the good things, son, not the bad."

Cindy looked at Mr. McCoy through narrowed eyes. He doesn't mean a word of it, she thought.

"I'd like a shot of you, sir, standing there against the Ferris wheel, with Sax," said Skip.

"Certainly," Mr. McCoy smiled. Skip's camera flashed. Jay and Dexter moved closer.

"How about one of Mr. McCoy sitting in one of the Ferris wheel cars?" Dexter asked.

"Right you are," Skip said. "If you would, sir?" he asked Mr. McCoy.

Mr. McCoy nodded and climbed into the car. Sax started the wheel, and the car with Mr. McCoy in it rose slowly.

Skip Bannerman said, "Headline reads 'Man About Town Is Child at Heart.' Or, let's see, 'Sky's the Limit for Carnival.'"

Mr. McCoy settled back in the Ferris wheel car. He smiled and waved.

Cindy felt sure that Mr. McCoy must be wondering how anyone had figured out all the mishaps at the carnival had been planned. He'd been so sure no one suspected him.

Skip lay on the ground, his camera poised. He fussed about focusing it. He said, "Same shot as I had before, Sax, only instead of Mrs. Darby and the little girl, I'll take Mr. McCoy."

Cindy darted over to Sax. She whispered, "Sax, this is very important. Get Mr. McCoy up to the top. Pretend something is wrong and keep him there."

Sax turned to Cindy, frowning. "I can't do that," he protested.

"You must do it, Sax, you must," Cindy insisted. "Just for ten minutes."

"I'm sorry, Cindy," he said, shaking his head. "I can't."

"For Marra, Sax," Cindy begged urgently.

Sax looked at her for a moment. Then he smiled. "If you say so." And he shifted the control on the Ferris wheel slightly.

10 · *One Last Surprise*

CINDY HURRIED over to Jay and Dexter. "He'll do it," she whispered. "Sax will keep McCoy up in the air."

They stared up. Mr. McCoy was leaning back easily, looking around at the carnival below.

"Now!" said Jay. "Let's go!"

"Wait!" Dexter said. "Remember Cindy said there's a guard at the warehouse."

"Cindy, you make up a story and get him out of the way," Jay suggested. "Then Dex and I can get in and look around."

Cindy nodded. "I'll tell the man Mr. McCoy has been hurt on the highway. I'll get him away from the warehouse. Don't worry."

"Okay, you go ahead," said Dexter. "We'll wait out of sight until we see you going off with him."

Cindy ran ahead. The boys saw her knock at the warehouse door. Then they saw her running toward the highway, the guard on her heels.

"Good for Cindy," Jay exclaimed.

"Now!" urged Dexter. He and Jay ran into the warehouse. They looked around them. There were stacks of boxes everywhere.

Dexter looked at the boxes. "Maybe these *are* stolen goods," he said. "But how can we tell the difference between stolen and unstolen?" He took his glasses off to wipe them on his shirt.

Walking along, still with his glasses in one hand, Dexter suddenly tripped. "I'm not all that clumsy," he said, putting his glasses on and looking down. "I tripped on something."

Jay wasn't paying attention to Dexter. He was saying, "I just hope Cindy can keep that guard away until we find something. And that she's all right," he added. "It would—"

"Look!" Dexter interrupted him. "It's a trap-door!" Jay hurried over to Dexter and stared at the floor.

Dexter knelt down. "Look," he said. "This floorboard is sticking up just a little. The trapdoor is flush with the floor. If it hadn't been just a little out of line I never would have seen it. Or tripped on it. Someone must have shut it in a hurry. Usually it would be invisible."

"How do we open it?" asked Jay.

"There must be some button or something," suggested Dexter. "But it looks like we'll have to find something to force it open."

Jay reached into his pocket and took out a scout knife. "Maybe we can get it up just enough so we can grab it," he said.

In a moment the boys had a grip on the edge. They pulled. The trapdoor opened slowly as they pulled. They propped it open and stared into the hole. Stairs stretched down into the darkness.

"We'll have to go down," said Dexter. "There must be a light switch here somewhere." He felt around. "Here." He flicked the switch, and the dark hole was lighted.

Dexter started down. Jay was right behind him.

"If only Cindy keeps the guard away," Jay said. "But what if—" He stopped and stared.

It was a big room, filled with tables. No one was in it. But there was what looked to Jay like an art shop or maybe a photographic darkroom or both. Then Jay grabbed Dexter. Stacked on the tables were small packages of twenty-dollar bills. Hundreds of small packages.

"Money!" Jay gasped. "McCoy must have robbed a bank!"

Dexter ran over and leaned down. He picked up one of the packages and examined it. Then he looked quickly at some of the equipment in the room.

"Counterfeit money," he said slowly. "McCoy must be running a counterfeiting operation here."

Suddenly he turned and started back up the stairs to the trapdoor. "We've got to call the police."

"I saw a phone upstairs in his office," Jay said.

The boys found the telephone quickly. "You call, Jay," said Dexter.

Jay picked up the telephone and dialed the

operator. "Please get me the police," he said. "This is an emergency."

Dexter stared at the telephone as Jay spoke. "Yes, this is an emergency. We need a squad car at the old McCoy warehouse on Highway 31 and Hathaway immediately. It's urgent."

He hung up and took a deep breath. "They'll radio a squad car right away," he said.

"Counterfeit money," breathed Dexter. "No wonder McCoy wanted to get the carnival out of the way. He didn't want anything here that would bring crowds of people. People might mean discovery, and he couldn't have that."

Minutes passed. "Where is Cindy?" Jay worried.

Suddenly there was the wailing sound of a siren. Dexter and Jay hurried to the door and stepped outside. They saw Cindy running toward them. The guard she had tricked away from the door was right behind her. Suddenly he stopped in his tracks. He stared at the flashing red lights of the approaching squad car, his face contorted with anger. And then he turned and ran.

Cindy's eyes were wide. "What's happened?

The police—" She stared at the boys.

"Counterfeit money!" Dexter said, breathless. "Under a trapdoor. It's a whole room for just making counterfeit money!"

The squad car suddenly screeched to a halt, its red lights flashing and spinning. Two policemen jumped out of the car and ran over to the Spotlighters. One of them was Hap Brady, the policeman the Spotlighters had met before.

"Hap Brady!" said Jay.

Hap Brady looked anxiously at the three detectives. "Are you kids okay? What's the emergency?"

"It's in the warehouse," Jay said. "Hurry."

"But wait," Cindy said urgently. "That man, the guard, he's running away! He's in on this, too." She pointed to a running figure. "You have to catch him!"

"I don't think I can do that," Hap Brady said. "I don't know what's—"

"You've got to trust us!" Dexter said desperately.

Hap Brady turned to his partner. "Get him, Bill," he said. The policeman ran after the fleeing man.

"Follow us," Jay said, hurrying into the warehouse.

Jay and Dexter led Cindy and the policeman through the large room to the trapdoor.

"It's down here," said Jay, leading the way down the hidden stairs.

Cindy gasped. "All that money!"

"Counterfeit money," Hap said wonderingly. He turned to the Spotlighters.

"What's going on? Who's doing this?"

"It's Mr. McCoy," Dexter said. "He's on the Park Committee and—"

"Where is he?" Hap interrupted.

"On top of the Ferris wheel," Cindy said.

"On top of the—" Hap Brady stared at Cindy.

"We asked Sax, he's the owner of the carnival, to keep him up there," said Dexter.

"Well, I'll be . . ." said Hap. "I wouldn't mind having you three on the force with me." Then he frowned. "We'll need more officers here. Right away. I'll put a call through on the radio. And then you three can lead me to this crook McCoy."

The policeman and the Spotlighters rushed upstairs and outside. Hap's partner was walking toward the squad car with the runaway guard.

"Bill, keep him in the car," Hap said. "And put in a call for more men. These kids here have just discovered a counterfeit operation."

Bill whistled and then said, "Right." He led the handcuffed guard to the back seat of the squad car and put his call through.

"Warehouse on 31 and Hathaway. This is an emergency call for more men. A counterfeit establishment has been discovered. Yes. On the double."

The three detectives and Hap Brady started running toward the Ferris wheel.

"McCoy," Hap said as he ran. "He's been on that Park Committee for nearly fifteen years now. And every time the community wanted something built out here, like a park, he voted against it. And no wonder. Making counterfeit money all these years," he said as they neared the Ferris wheel.

As the Spotlighters and Hap Brady reached the Ferris wheel, sirens sounded in the distance. In a moment the whole carnival seemed surrounded by flashing red lights from squad cars.

"What's happening?" Sax asked anxiously, standing at the controls of the Ferris wheel.

127

"Don't worry, Sax," said Cindy. "Everything's all right. I promise."

She glanced around. Crowds had gathered. Some people were looking in bewilderment at the flashing lights of the police cars pulling up to the entrance of the carnival. Some were looking up at the top of the Ferris wheel.

Cindy looked up, too. Mr. McCoy was waving his arms and shouting. But his words were lost in the other noises.

Marra ran over to Sax. She cried, "Darling Sax, don't worry! Something is happening, but it has good vibes. I know it does!"

The news spread like wildfire through the crowd. Skip Bannerman stood taking pictures, of McCoy high in the air, of the crowds, of the police. Then he beckoned to Jay, Dexter, and Cindy. "Now a picture of you three, if you please. Smile. You have a very good reason to. Ready?"

The flash went off. " 'Kids Catch Crook at Keyhole Carnival,' " he said. "Perfect."